The Day Jake Vacuumed

Timmy the cat

This Jake book
belongs to

.... Kira ....

To Tricia, Mike,
Yasmin and Natasha
– with love

This edition first published 2002 by
Walker Books Ltd, 87 Vauxhall Walk, London SE11 5HJ

10 9 8 7 6 5 4 3 2 1

© 1989, 2002 Simon James

The right of Simon James to be identified as author of this
work has been asserted by him in accordance with the Copyright,
Designs and Patents Act 1988

This book has been typeset in Usherwood ITC

Printed in Hong Kong

British Library Cataloguing in Publication Data: a catalogue record for this book
is available from the British Library

ISBN 0-7445-9400-6

The Day
Jake
Vacuumed

Simon James

WALKER BOOKS
AND SUBSIDIARIES
LONDON • BOSTON • SYDNEY

Jake was difficult.
Jake was a problem.
He didn't like doing
anything for anyone.

So you can imagine how Jake felt when
one day his mother asked him to do the
vacuum cleaning.
For a while, Jake played with the machine,
enjoying the loud noise it made.

Then a really wicked idea occurred to him.
Very quietly he crept over to Timmy, the cat.
Aiming the nozzle at Timmy, Jake switched on
the vacuum cleaner and sucked up the poor cat!
Jake was delighted.

Jake knew he would be in trouble.
I might as well make it BIG TROUBLE! thought Jake.
He sneaked off to the kitchen …

and sucked his mother up into the
vacuum cleaner, rubber gloves and all!

"Yippee. I'm free!" shouted Jake.
"No one to tell me to do anything!"
He had the whole house to himself,
except, that is, for his sister upstairs.

Jake's sister was in her bedroom,
playing with her dolls.
In crept Jake.
He climbed on top of the cupboard
and switched on the vacuum cleaner.
You can imagine what happened then.

But, oh dear! Jake remembered
that his father would be home soon.
There was only one thing to do.

At six o'clock on the dot, Jake's father opened
the front door. Out jumped Jake with the
vacuum cleaner roaring on full power.
It was a difficult fit at first, but eventually …
POP! In went Jake's father.
"Hooray!" shouted Jake.

Jake was delighted.
At last he was in charge!
He was so pleased that he decided to
suck up the WHOLE room, and indeed,
the whole page of this book …

leaving only himself and the vacuum
cleaner. Jake was free.

But Jake hadn't noticed that the vacuum cleaner was now stuffed to bursting point and about to explode.

And explode it did, with a gigantic bang!
Once Jake's parents had recovered, they were furious.
They sent him to bed early – without any supper.

But Jake didn't mind. At least he knew he would never ever be asked to do the vacuuming again.